Get
Money
Girls

Rachael Reed
©2024

Get Money Girls
By Rachael Reed

Chapter 1: The Struggle is Real

The sun barely peeked over the horizon as the Reed sisters—Isis, Bria, Asia, and Nikki—woke up to another day in the unforgiving streets of the ghetto. Their two-bedroom apartment, crammed with worn-out furniture and hand-me-downs, was a stark reminder of their daily struggle. Their hardworking mother, Ms. Reed, had already left for her early morning shift at the diner, leaving behind a note on the fridge reminding her daughters to stay strong and stick together.

Isis, the eldest at twenty-one, had taken on the role of the second mother. She stood at the cracked mirror in the bathroom, trying to make herself look presentable for her job at the corner store. Her long braids, tied back with a bright scarf, framed her tired yet determined face. "Yo, Bria! Get up, we gotta hustle today!" she called out, her voice carrying the weight of responsibility.

Bria, a fiery eighteen-year-old with a passion for art, groaned as she rolled out of bed. "Man, I hate this place. One day, I'ma get us outta here, you'll see," she muttered, grabbing her sketchbook and pencils. Her dreams of becoming an artist were her escape from the harsh reality of their environment.

Asia, the quiet one, was sixteen and already wise beyond her years. She shuffled into the kitchen, her eyes heavy with the fatigue of staying up late to study. "Nikki, you got breakfast ready?" she asked, glancing at her thirteen-year-old sister who was busy scrambling eggs in their tiny, outdated kitchen.

"Yeah, almost done," Nikki replied, her bright eyes contrasting with the worn expression on her young face. She was the baby of the family but had learned quickly how to fend for herself and help out where she could.

Their neighborhood was a battleground, a place where hope and despair coexisted in a fragile balance. The sound of sirens and gunshots was as common as the laughter of children playing in the streets.

Graffiti-covered walls told stories of lost youth and forgotten dreams. The sisters knew all too well the dangers lurking around every corner—gang violence, drug dealers, and the ever-present threat of poverty.

As they sat down for a quick breakfast, Isis looked around at her sisters, her heart aching with a mix of love and frustration. "We gotta stick together, y'all. Mom's doing everything she can, but we gotta pull our weight too," she said, her voice firm.

"Man, I hate this life," Bria repeated, her eyes filled with a mix of anger and sadness. "I wanna be somebody, not just another girl from the hood."

Asia nodded, her gaze distant. "We will, Bria. We just gotta play it smart and keep our heads up."

Nikki chimed in, her voice small but determined. "We got each other. That's all that matters."

The sisters finished their breakfast and prepared to face the day. Isis grabbed her purse and headed out, her mind already racing with the challenges she knew lay ahead. Bria stayed behind for a few minutes, sketching furiously before she had to leave for school. Asia packed her books, determined to ace her exams and earn a scholarship. Nikki cleaned up the kitchen, her thoughts drifting to the safety of her sisters.

As Isis walked down the cracked sidewalk, she couldn't help but notice the boarded-up windows and trash-strewn streets. This was their reality, a world where survival was a daily battle. She passed by groups of young men hanging out on the corners, their eyes hard and wary. She knew most of them, had grown up with them, but now their paths had diverged.

"Hey, Isis!" a voice called out. She turned to see Trey, a local hustler with a reputation for trouble. "You good?"

Isis forced a smile. "Yeah, Trey, just trying to make it through the day, you know?"

Trey nodded, his eyes scanning the street for any signs of danger. "I feel you. Stay safe out here."

As Isis continued on her way, she thought about the choices she and her sisters faced every day. The lure of easy money was always there, but so was the cost—jail, addiction, or worse. She was determined to keep her family on the straight and narrow, even if it meant sacrificing her own dreams.

Back at the apartment, Bria finished her sketch and headed to school, her mind filled with visions of a better future. She saw herself in a studio, creating art that would inspire others and lift her family out of the ghetto. Asia walked beside her, her focus on her studies and the promise of a scholarship that could change her life. Nikki stayed behind, her young mind grappling with the harsh realities of their world.

The Reed sisters were fighters, each in their own way. They faced a world that was often unforgiving, but they had each other, and that made all the difference. Their dreams and aspirations were the light that guided them through the darkness, a beacon of hope in a world that desperately needed it.

As the day unfolded, each sister faced their own battles, but they knew they were stronger together. They were determined to rise above their circumstances, to break free from the cycle of poverty and violence that had trapped so many before them. The struggle was real, but so was their resolve. And in the heart of the ghetto, the Reed sisters fought for their dreams, one day at a time.

Chapter 2: Tragedy Strikes

The day started like any other for the Reed sisters, but it quickly turned into their worst nightmare. Isis was at work, stocking shelves at the corner store, when her phone rang. The frantic voice on the other end was Nikki, barely holding back tears.

"Isis, you gotta come home. It's Mama. She ain't moving, and she ain't talkin' right," Nikki choked out, her voice trembling.

Isis felt a cold wave of fear wash over her. "What happened? Is she breathing? Call 911 right now!" she shouted, dropping everything and rushing out of the store.

By the time Isis reached their apartment, an ambulance was already there. Paramedics were lifting Ms. Reed onto a stretcher, her face slack and unresponsive. The sisters huddled together, their faces pale with shock and fear. Isis felt her heart pounding in her chest, each beat echoing the terror that gripped her.

"She had a stroke," one of the paramedics said, his tone grim. "We're taking her to County General."

Isis nodded, her throat tight with emotion. "We'll be right behind you," she managed to say, her voice barely a whisper.

The ride to the hospital felt like an eternity. In the waiting room, the sisters clung to each other, their minds racing with worst-case scenarios. Asia, usually the calm and collected one, was shaking. Bria stared blankly at the floor, her eyes filled with unshed tears. Nikki was sobbing quietly, her small frame trembling with fear.

A doctor finally emerged, his expression serious. "Your mother had a severe stroke. She's stable for now, but her condition is critical. We need to run more tests to determine the extent of the damage."

The sisters nodded numbly, trying to process the doctor's words. They were allowed to see their mother briefly. The sight of her lying motionless, hooked up to machines, was almost too much to bear. Her strong, resilient spirit seemed so far away now, replaced by a frail body struggling to hold on.

Isis took a deep breath, trying to be strong for her sisters. "We gonna get through this, y'all. Mama's a fighter, and so are we."

The next few days were a blur of hospital visits, consultations, and grim news. The doctors explained that Ms. Reed would need extensive therapy and treatments to recover, and even then, there were no guarantees. The sisters quickly realized the enormity of the financial burden they faced. Without health insurance, the medical bills piled up fast, each one a stark reminder of their desperate situation.

Isis took on extra shifts at the corner store, working late into the night and coming home exhausted. Asia, who was supposed to be focusing on her studies, found herself juggling school and part-time jobs to help out. Bria sold her artwork on the streets, hoping to scrape together enough money to contribute. Nikki, too young to work legally, did odd jobs for neighbors, anything to bring in a little cash.

One evening, Isis gathered her sisters in the living room, their faces illuminated by the dim light of a single lamp. "We gotta talk about how we gonna pay these bills. Mama's therapy alone costs more than we make in a month."

Bria, her face drawn and tired, looked up. "Maybe we can get a loan or somethin'."

Asia shook her head. "Ain't nobody gonna give us a loan, Bria. We barely got enough credit to buy groceries."

Nikki, tears streaming down her face, spoke up. "What if we... what if we ask for help? There's gotta be someone who can help us."

Isis sighed, the weight of their reality pressing down on her. "We can try, but we gotta be prepared for the worst. We might need to make some hard choices."

The sisters fell silent, each lost in their own thoughts. They knew the streets held opportunities, but those came with risks. Easy money often led to hard consequences, and they had seen too many lives destroyed by the same temptations that now loomed over them.

A few days later, as Isis was leaving the hospital, she ran into Trey, the local hustler. He noticed the dark circles under her eyes and the worry etched into her face. "Hey, Isis. You good?"

Isis hesitated, then decided to confide in him. "Nah, Trey. Mama had a stroke. We ain't got insurance, and the bills are killin' us."

Trey's expression softened. "Damn, that's rough. Look, if you need some extra cash, I might know a way."

Isis knew what he was implying, and the thought made her stomach churn. "I appreciate it, Trey, but we ain't about that life."

Trey nodded, respect in his eyes. "I get it. But if you change your mind, you know where to find me."

The sisters continued to fight against the mounting pressure, their bond growing stronger with each passing day. They sold what little they had of value, reached out to every charity and assistance program they could find, and even considered starting a crowdfunding campaign. But despite their best efforts, the financial strain only seemed to grow.

One night, as they gathered around the dinner table, Isis spoke up. "I been thinkin'. We gotta find a way to make real money, fast. Maybe we could start a legit business or somethin'."

Asia looked skeptical. "And where we gonna get the money to start a business, Isis? We can barely keep the lights on."

Bria, her eyes filled with determination, said, "Maybe we gotta take a chance. Do somethin' bold. We can't keep livin' like this."

Nikki nodded, her youthful face set with resolve. "Whatever it takes, we gotta do it. For Mama."

The sisters knew they were standing at a crossroads. The choices they made in the coming days would determine their future, for better or worse. As they sat together, they felt a renewed sense of purpose. They were ready to fight, to sacrifice, and to do whatever it took to save their mother and themselves.

The struggle was real, but so was their resolve. In the heart of the ghetto, amidst the darkness and despair, the Reed sisters were ready to rise above their circumstances and forge a new path. The road ahead was uncertain, fraught with danger and challenges, but they were determined to face it together, no matter what.

Chapter 3: Desperate Times

The air in the small apartment was thick with tension. The Reed sisters sat around their rickety kitchen table, faces etched with worry and exhaustion. The ticking of the clock on the wall was the only sound breaking the heavy silence. They were at a breaking point, and it was time to figure out how to pull themselves out of the hole they were in.

Isis, the eldest, leaned back in her chair, rubbing her temples. "Alright, y'all, we gotta come up with somethin'. We need money, and we need it fast. Mama ain't gettin' better without that therapy, and we can't keep drownin' in these bills."

Bria, her arms crossed and eyes red from crying, nodded. "Yeah, but what can we do? Ain't nobody gonna lend us that kinda money, and I ain't tryin' to go beggin.'"

Asia, always the practical one, pulled out a notepad. "We gotta brainstorm. Legal and... not so legal. We need options."

Nikki, the youngest, sat quietly, her eyes darting around the room. She had her own problems, but now wasn't the time to bring them up. "I got a couple ideas, but they ain't exactly on the up and up," she muttered.

Isis sighed. "Let's hear 'em. We ain't in a position to be picky right now."

Nikki took a deep breath. "Well, we could look into some side hustles. You know, sellin' stuff online, maybe some freelance work. But that ain't gonna bring in the kinda money we need. We could also... hit some spots. Robbery."

The room fell silent. The thought of turning to crime was a heavy one, but desperation had a way of pushing people to extremes.

Bria spoke up, her voice trembling. "You talkin' 'bout robbin' people? Like, straight up takin' what we need?"

Nikki nodded, her face serious. "Yeah. We target the rich folks. The ones who ain't gonna miss a few thousand. We get in, get out, and nobody gets hurt."

Isis rubbed her forehead, her mind racing. "That's risky, Nikki. We get caught, we goin' to prison. And we ain't exactly got a crew of professionals."

Asia flipped through her notepad, jotting down ideas. "We need to consider all our options. Legal means ain't gettin' us nowhere fast enough. We could start small, maybe look for some scams or hustles that ain't too dangerous."

Isis leaned forward, her face hardening with determination. "Aight, let's break it down. What else we got?"

Bria looked up, her eyes dark with anger. "We could sell some of my art. I know it ain't much, but I got connections. Maybe we could make some quick cash."

Asia nodded, adding it to the list. "What about you, Isis? You got any connects that could help us out?"

Isis hesitated. "Well, there is one thing. Remember Kev? My baby daddy? He owe me big time, and he's been doin' pretty well for himself. We could lean on him for some help."

Nikki's eyes widened. "You serious? You really think he gonna help us out after all the drama y'all had?"

Isis shrugged. "It's worth a shot. Desperate times, remember?"

As they brainstormed, the sisters' individual problems began to surface. Isis's relationship with Kev had always been tumultuous, filled with fights and betrayal. Now, with their mother sick and the bills piling up, she had no choice but to swallow her pride and reach out to him.

Bria, on the other hand, was trapped in an abusive relationship with Marcus, a local thug who controlled her every move. She had dreams of becoming an artist, but Marcus kept her on a tight leash, using violence and manipulation to keep her in line.

Asia was struggling to balance school and work. She was determined to get her degree and lift her family out of poverty, but the demands of both were wearing her down. She knew she couldn't keep this up forever, and something had to give.

And then there was Nikki, the youngest, who had recently had a run-in with the law. She had been caught shoplifting, trying to bring home some essentials for her family. Now, she was facing juvenile detention and the threat of a criminal record.

Isis looked around the table, her eyes filled with determination. "We all got our issues, but we gotta stay focused. We need to make a plan and stick to it. No more messin' around. This is about Mama, and we ain't lettin' her down."

The sisters nodded, their resolve strengthening. They knew the road ahead was dangerous, but they were willing to take the risk. They had each other, and they were ready to fight for their family.

As the days passed, the idea of robbery began to take shape. They started small, casing potential targets and gathering information. They knew the risks, but desperation pushed them forward. They couldn't afford to fail.

One evening, Isis met with Kev, her heart pounding in her chest. She explained their situation, the dire need for money, and the possibility of robbing wealthy targets. Kev listened, his expression unreadable.

"I'll help you out, Isis," he finally said. "But you gotta be careful. This ain't no game. You get caught, and it's over."

Isis nodded, her eyes hard. "I know. We ain't got no other choice."

Back at the apartment, the sisters continued to plan. They knew they were stepping into dangerous territory, but their love for their mother and their desire to escape the ghetto drove them forward. They would do whatever it took to save their family, even if it meant crossing lines they never thought they would.

The struggle was real, but so was their determination. The Reed sisters were ready to face the challenges ahead, no matter the cost. Their journey was just beginning, and the path they chose would define their future.

Chapter 4: The Plan

The air in the apartment was thick with tension as the Reed sisters huddled around the kitchen table. The sound of the city outside, with its sirens and distant shouts, served as a constant reminder of the world they were trying to survive in. They were about to step into a new level of danger, and every decision they made had to be perfect.

Isis spread out a map of the neighborhood, marking specific locations with a red marker. "Aight, we gotta do this right. We ain't got no room for mistakes. Our target is Mr. Klein. Rich dude, lives in that big-ass house on Elm Street. He's got money, jewels, and we know he's got a safe full of cash."

Bria, leaning over the table with a serious expression, nodded. "How we gonna get in? Dude's probably got security."

Nikki, ever the resourceful one, grinned. "I been watchin'. He's got one guard, but he's lazy. Spends more time on his phone than watchin' the house. Plus, there's a side door that ain't as secure. That's our way in."

Asia, quiet and thoughtful, added, "We need to know his schedule. When he's home, when he ain't. We can't just barge in without knowin' when it's safe."

Isis looked around the table, her eyes filled with determination. "I been keepin' track. He goes out every Thursday night to that fancy club downtown. We hit him then, when the house is empty. We got one hour, tops."

The sisters exchanged nervous glances. They knew the risks. One mistake could land them in jail or worse. But the stakes were high, and their mother's life depended on their success.

"Here's how it's gonna go down," Isis continued, her voice steady. "Nikki, you handle the door. You got them skills with the locks. Bria, you keep watch. Make sure nobody sees us goin' in or out. Asia, you find the safe. I'll crack it. We grab what we can and get out."

Bria chewed her lip, her mind racing. "What if somethin' goes wrong? We need a backup plan."

Isis nodded. "If we get caught, we run. Split up, head to the safe house on 4th Street. We meet back here after. Nobody talks, nobody gets caught."

The gravity of the situation weighed heavily on them. They were about to cross a line, stepping into a world of crime that could destroy everything they were trying to save. But desperation had a way of pushing people to extremes, and they were ready to do whatever it took.

The next few days were a blur of preparation. They gathered tools, mapped out escape routes, and rehearsed their roles. The tension in the apartment was palpable, each sister dealing with their own fears and anxieties in their own way.

Isis, the backbone of the family, stayed strong. She knew she had to lead by example, even though the thought of what they were about to do made her stomach churn. She spent hours practicing with the tools Kev had given her, determined not to fail.

Bria, haunted by the abuse from Marcus, threw herself into the planning. This was her way out, her chance to take control of her life. She was done being a victim, and she was ready to fight for her family.

Asia, balancing school and work, used her intelligence to plan every detail. She knew the risks but saw no other option. Her dreams of a better life fueled her determination to make this heist a success.

Nikki, the youngest, was both excited and terrified. She had always been resourceful, finding ways to survive in the harshest conditions. This was just another challenge, another way to prove herself. But deep down, she knew the stakes had never been higher.

The night of the heist arrived. The sisters dressed in black, their faces set with grim determination. They moved like shadows through the streets, sticking to the plan they had rehearsed so many times.

As they approached Mr. Klein's mansion, the reality of what they were about to do hit them hard. The house loomed before them, a symbol of wealth and power, everything they had never had.

Nikki took a deep breath and got to work on the side door. Her hands shook slightly, but she forced herself to focus. Within minutes, the lock clicked open. "We're in," she whispered, her voice barely audible.

Bria took her position outside, her eyes scanning the street for any signs of trouble. Asia and Isis slipped inside, their hearts pounding in their chests. They moved quickly, knowing they had a limited window before Mr. Klein returned.

Asia found the safe in the study, just as they had planned. She motioned to Isis, who pulled out the tools and got to work. The seconds ticked by, each one feeling like an eternity.

Outside, Bria's heart raced as a car slowed down near the house. She held her breath, ready to signal her sisters if things went south. But the car moved on, and she exhaled in relief.

Inside, Isis finally cracked the safe. The door swung open, revealing stacks of cash and a collection of expensive jewelry. She quickly stuffed the money and valuables into a bag, her hands trembling with a mix of fear and excitement.

"Let's go," she whispered, and they made their way back to the door, careful not to make a sound.

As they slipped out of the house, Bria joined them, and they moved swiftly through the streets, sticking to the shadows. They didn't breathe easy until they were back in their apartment, the door locked behind them.

They emptied the bag onto the kitchen table, the sight of the money and jewels almost surreal. They had done it. They had pulled off the heist. But the relief was short-lived, replaced by the sobering reality of what they had just done.

"This is just the beginning," Isis said, her voice steady. "We gotta be smart. This money will help, but we can't get reckless. We gotta take care of Mama, and we gotta stay outta jail."

The sisters nodded, their bond stronger than ever. They had taken a dangerous step, but they were ready to face whatever came next. Together, they would fight for their family, no matter the cost.

The struggle was real, but so was their resolve. In the heart of the ghetto, amidst the darkness and danger, the Reed sisters were determined to rise above their circumstances and carve out a new path. The road ahead was uncertain, but they would face it together, ready for whatever challenges lay ahead.

Chapter 5: The First Heist

The night was thick with tension as the Reed sisters approached Mr. Klein's mansion. The adrenaline coursing through their veins made every sound seem amplified—the distant sirens, the hum of streetlights, the crunch of gravel under their shoes. They were about to cross a line that could change their lives forever, and there was no turning back.

Isis, the oldest and the leader of the group, took a deep breath and whispered, "Aight, y'all. This is it. Stick to the plan, and we get in and out clean. Nikki, you got the door?"

Nikki, the youngest but already skilled with a lock pick, nodded. "Yeah, I got it. Just give me a sec."

The side door to the mansion was supposed to be their easiest point of entry. Nikki worked quickly, her fingers deftly manipulating the tools. She could hear her heart pounding in her ears, the weight of the moment pressing down on her. After what felt like an eternity, the lock clicked open.

"Got it," she whispered, pushing the door open.

Isis and Asia slipped inside, followed by Bria, who took her position outside as the lookout. The interior of the mansion was dimly lit, casting long shadows that seemed to dance with every step they took. They moved quickly but cautiously, their senses on high alert.

Asia led the way to the study, where the safe was hidden behind a large painting. She glanced at Isis, who nodded and pulled out her tools. Isis had practiced cracking the safe for days, but now, under the pressure, her hands shook.

"Keep it together, Isis," she muttered to herself, focusing on the task at hand. The clicks of the tumblers falling into place were the only sounds in the room.

Outside, Bria scanned the street nervously. A car slowed as it passed the mansion, and she held her breath, ready to signal her sisters if needed.

The car moved on, and she exhaled in relief, but her heart continued to race.

Inside, Isis finally got the safe open. The sight of stacks of cash and glittering jewels was almost surreal. They quickly stuffed everything into bags, their movements quick and efficient.

"We got what we need. Let's go," Isis whispered.

They moved back towards the door, but just as they were about to step outside, they heard the unmistakable sound of footsteps. The guard, who had been napping in the security booth, was making his rounds.

"Shit," Nikki hissed. "What do we do?"

"Stay calm," Isis ordered. "We wait for him to pass, then we move."

The guard's flashlight beam cut through the darkness, inches from where they were hiding. They held their breath, their hearts pounding as they waited. After what felt like an eternity, the guard moved on, and they slipped out the door.

Bria joined them, and they moved quickly but quietly through the backyard, sticking to the shadows. They were almost to the fence when they heard the sound of a car engine revving. A police cruiser turned onto the street, its headlights sweeping across the yard.

"Run!" Isis yelled, her voice low but urgent.

They bolted, the adrenaline pushing them forward. They scaled the fence, their bags of loot clinking as they landed on the other side. The police car slowed, and they ducked into an alley, pressing themselves against the wall, praying they wouldn't be seen.

The cruiser paused, the officer inside seemingly oblivious to the four girls hidden in the shadows. After a moment, the car continued down the street, and they let out the breath they had been holding.

"That was too close," Asia whispered, her voice trembling.

"We ain't outta the woods yet," Isis replied. "Let's move."

They ran through the alleyways, sticking to the darkest paths, until they reached their safe house on 4th Street. Only when the door was securely locked behind them did they allow themselves to collapse on the floor, panting from the exertion and the adrenaline rush.

For a moment, they were silent, the reality of what they had just done sinking in. Then, Nikki started to laugh, a sound of pure relief and exhilaration. The others joined in, their laughter tinged with disbelief and triumph.

"We did it," Bria said, her eyes wide with amazement. "We actually did it."

Isis grinned, pulling the bags into the center of the room. "Let's see what we got."

They opened the bags, the sight of the money and jewels almost blinding in its brilliance. They had hit the jackpot, and for the first time in their lives, they felt a glimmer of hope.

"This is just the beginning," Isis said, her voice filled with determination. "We gonna take care of Mama, and we gonna get outta this life. But we gotta be smart. We can't get reckless."

Asia nodded, her mind already racing with plans for the future. "We need to lay low for a while. Keep our heads down and act like everything's normal."

Bria, her face flushed with excitement, said, "And we gotta keep this between us. Nobody else can know. Not even Kev."

Nikki, still catching her breath, looked around at her sisters. "We in this together. Ride or die."

They sat there for a while, basking in their success, the adrenaline slowly fading. They knew the risks they had taken, and the danger was far from over. But for now, they had a chance. A chance to change their lives, to rise above the circumstances that had held them down for so long.

As the first light of dawn began to creep through the windows, the Reed sisters knew they had taken their first step into a new world. A world filled with danger and uncertainty, but also with the promise of a better future. They had tasted the thrill of success, and there was no turning back.

The struggle was real, but so was their resolve. In the heart of the ghetto, amidst the darkness and danger, the Reed sisters were ready to fight for their dreams, no matter the cost. The road ahead was long and treacherous, but they were ready to face it together, ready to take on whatever challenges lay ahead.

Chapter 6: The Aftermath

The initial rush of adrenaline had faded, leaving the Reed sisters in a mix of elation and unease. They sat around the kitchen table in their cramped apartment, the bags of cash and jewels spread out before them like a twisted treasure trove. The success of their first heist was undeniable, but the reality of what they had done was starting to sink in.

Isis, the leader, stared at the pile of money, her mind racing with conflicting thoughts. "We did it," she said, her voice barely above a whisper. "We really did it."

Bria, still buzzing from the excitement, laughed nervously. "Hell yeah, we did. This is more money than we ever seen in our lives."

Asia, always the thinker, looked troubled. "Yeah, but at what cost? We broke the law, y'all. We coulda got caught. We coulda went to jail."

Nikki, the youngest, tried to lighten the mood. "But we didn't. We pulled it off. Now we can take care of Mama and maybe even get outta here."

The sisters' celebration was short-lived. The reality of their actions began to weigh heavily on them. They had crossed a line, and there was no going back. The money and jewels represented a chance at a better life, but they also symbolized the danger and moral ambiguity they now faced.

Isis sighed, her face etched with worry. "We gotta be careful. We can't get reckless. We gotta stay smart and keep our heads down."

Bria nodded, but her eyes were still shining with the thrill of their success. "I get that, but we did what we had to do. Ain't nobody gonna give us nothin'. We gotta take what's ours."

Asia frowned, her conscience gnawing at her. "But is this who we wanna be? Thieves? Criminals? We ain't got no other options?"

Isis looked at her younger sister, understanding her concerns. "We gotta do what we gotta do, Asia. This money is gonna help Mama, and it's gonna help us. We just gotta be smart about it."

The sisters fell into a contemplative silence, each wrestling with their own thoughts and feelings. They knew they had to stay united, but the moral and ethical dilemmas of their actions were starting to create cracks in their plan.

As the days passed, the tension in the apartment grew. The sisters tried to go about their daily routines, but the heist weighed heavily on their minds. They couldn't shake the feeling that someone was watching them, that the law was closing in.

One evening, as they gathered for dinner, Bria voiced her concerns. "I think someone saw us. I been feelin' like we bein' watched."

Isis looked up sharply. "You serious? You see anyone followin' you?"

Bria shook her head. "Not exactly. Just a feeling. Like, I seen this car pass by the house a few times, and it just feels off."

Asia's anxiety spiked. "We can't afford to get caught, y'all. We gotta lay low and be extra careful."

Nikki, trying to stay positive, said, "Maybe it's just nerves. We did somethin' big, and it's normal to feel paranoid."

Isis nodded, but the worry in her eyes was evident. "We gotta trust each other and stay alert. If any of us feels somethin' ain't right, we speak up."

The sisters agreed, but the unease lingered. They had stepped into a dangerous game, and the stakes were higher than they had ever imagined.

One night, while they were sorting through the loot, Nikki noticed something that made her blood run cold. "Hey, y'all. Look at this," she said, holding up a necklace.

The necklace was beautiful, adorned with diamonds and rubies, but it was also unmistakably unique. It had been in the local news recently, reported stolen from a high-profile socialite.

Bria's eyes widened. "Oh shit. That necklace is hot. We can't sell that. It's gonna get traced back to us."

Isis cursed under her breath. "Damn it. We gotta get rid of it. We can't afford to have any links to that heist."

Asia, ever the pragmatist, suggested, "We could break it down, sell the stones separately. It won't be as much, but it's safer."

The sisters agreed, but the incident only heightened their paranoia. They realized how precarious their situation was and how easily their success could turn into disaster.

As the weeks went by, the sisters continued to wrestle with the moral implications of their actions. They knew they had done what was necessary to survive, but the cost was becoming more apparent.

Isis struggled with her role as the leader, trying to balance the need for money with the safety and well-being of her family. She felt the weight of their actions on her shoulders, knowing that any misstep could destroy everything they had worked for.

Bria found herself increasingly troubled by the violence and danger of their new life. Her abusive relationship with Marcus added another layer of stress, as he became suspicious of her sudden change in behavior and financial situation.

Asia tried to maintain her focus on school, but the guilt and fear gnawed at her. She wanted to believe they were doing the right thing, but the lines between right and wrong were becoming blurred.

Nikki, the youngest, struggled to reconcile her excitement with the harsh reality of their actions. She had always been resourceful, but now she was dealing with a level of danger and morality that she had never faced before.

The sisters knew they had to stay united, but the cracks in their plan were starting to show. Trust and communication became more important than ever as they navigated the treacherous path they had chosen.

One evening, as they gathered to discuss their next move, Isis looked at her sisters with determination. "We gotta stick together. No matter what happens, we gotta have each other's backs. We did this for Mama, and we gotta see it through."

The sisters nodded, their resolve strengthening. They had made their choice, and there was no turning back. They would face the dangers and challenges ahead with courage and unity, ready to fight for their family and their future.

The struggle was real, but so was their determination. In the heart of the ghetto, amidst the darkness and danger, the Reed sisters were ready to rise above their circumstances and forge a new path. The road ahead was uncertain, but they would face it together, ready to take on whatever challenges lay ahead.

Chapter 7: Escalating Stakes

The success of their first heist had given the Reed sisters a taste of what was possible, but it also heightened their hunger for more. The money they had stolen was helping with their mother's medical bills, but it wasn't enough to secure their future. They needed another score, and this time, they aimed higher.

Isis called a meeting in their apartment, the tension palpable. "Aight, y'all. We did good last time, but we gotta think bigger. We need another hit, and it needs to be bigger."

Bria leaned in, her face serious. "What you got in mind?"

Isis spread out a blueprint on the table. "There's a jewelry store downtown, real high-end. Security's tight, but if we plan it right, we can pull it off."

Asia raised an eyebrow. "A jewelry store? That's risky. Cops gonna be all over that."

Isis nodded. "I know, but the payoff is worth it. We need the money, and this is our shot."

Nikki, ever the adventurous one, grinned. "I'm down. What's the plan?"

As they hashed out the details, the sisters knew they were stepping into more dangerous territory. The stakes were higher, and the risks greater, but desperation drove them forward.

The next day, Isis met up with Kev at a local diner. He had connections and could help them with the logistics. Kev listened intently as Isis laid out the plan, his face serious.

"That's a big score, Isis. You sure y'all can handle it?" Kev asked, his eyes narrowing.

Isis nodded. "We ain't got no choice. We need this money."

Kev sighed. "Aight. I got some people who can help. They'll provide the tools and the getaway car, but y'all need to be careful. Cops are on high alert after that last hit."

Back at the apartment, new characters began to enter the sisters' lives. Tasha, an old friend of Bria's, joined the crew. She was street-smart and had experience in heists, making her a valuable addition. Marcus, Bria's abusive boyfriend, grew suspicious of her activities and became an unpredictable variable.

As the sisters finalized their plan, the tension in the city grew. Law enforcement had intensified their search for the robbers, and the streets were buzzing with rumors. The pressure was on, and the sisters felt it with every passing day.

One evening, while the sisters were going over their plan, Tasha brought in a new face. "This is Rico. He's a tech wiz. Can hack into security systems, disable alarms, you name it."

Isis sized up Rico, her eyes cautious. "You sure we can trust him?"

Tasha nodded. "He's solid. We need him for this job."

Rico, a wiry man with sharp eyes, nodded. "I got y'all covered. Just tell me what you need."

With Rico on board, the plan began to take shape. They would hit the jewelry store at closing time, when the security was changing shifts. Rico would disable the alarms, and the sisters would get in and out quickly.

As the day of the heist approached, the sisters felt the pressure mounting. They knew the risks, but they also knew they had no other choice. Their mother's health depended on them, and failure was not an option.

The night before the heist, Isis gathered the crew for a final briefing. "Aight, y'all. This is it. We stick to the plan, we stay focused, and we get out clean. No mistakes."

Bria, her face set with determination, nodded. "We got this."

Asia, always the cautious one, added, "Remember, if anything goes wrong, we abort. No heroics."

Nikki, her eyes shining with excitement, grinned. "Let's do this."

The day of the heist arrived, and the sisters were ready. They dressed in black, their faces set with grim determination. Rico set up in a van outside the jewelry store, his fingers flying over the keyboard as he hacked into the security system.

"Alarms are down," Rico said through their earpieces. "You're good to go."

Isis, Bria, and Nikki slipped into the store, moving quickly and efficiently. Asia stayed outside, keeping watch. The interior of the store was dimly lit, the glass cases filled with glittering jewels.

"Move fast," Isis whispered, her voice tense.

They began stuffing jewels into their bags, their movements quick and precise. The adrenaline coursing through their veins made every second feel like an eternity.

Outside, Asia saw a police car turn onto the street. "Cops are coming. You got two minutes, tops."

Isis's heart pounded as she grabbed the last of the jewels. "We're almost done. Let's move."

They made their way to the back door, their bags heavy with loot. As they stepped outside, the sound of sirens filled the air. The police were closing in.

"Run!" Isis shouted, and they bolted for the getaway car.

Rico was waiting, the engine running. They piled into the car, their hearts racing as the sirens grew louder. Rico floored the gas pedal, the tires screeching as they sped away.

The police car turned the corner just as they disappeared into the night. For a moment, it seemed like they had made it, but then the reality of their situation hit them. They were on the run, and the law was hot on their trail.

As they sped through the city streets, Isis looked at her sisters. "We did it, but we gotta lay low. The cops ain't gonna stop looking for us."

Bria nodded, her face pale but determined. "We got what we needed. Now we just gotta stay outta sight."

Asia, her mind racing with fear and adrenaline, said, "We can't go back home. We need a new safe house."

Nikki, still buzzing with excitement, grinned. "We'll find a place. We always do."

The sisters knew they had crossed a line, and there was no turning back. The stakes were higher, and the danger more real than ever. They had tasted the thrill of success, but they also felt the weight of their choices.

As they drove into the night, the city lights flickering around them, they knew they were in deeper than ever. The road ahead was uncertain, but they were ready to face it together, ready to fight for their family and their future.

The struggle was real, but so was their resolve. In the heart of the ghetto, amidst the darkness and danger, the Reed sisters were determined to rise above their circumstances and carve out a new path. The stakes were escalating, and the game was more dangerous than ever, but they were ready to face whatever came next.

Chapter 8: Betrayal and Trust

The aftermath of the heist left the Reed sisters on edge. They had pulled off the job and escaped the law, but the tension among them was palpable. The thrill of the heist had worn off, replaced by a simmering anxiety that threatened to tear them apart.

Isis sat at the kitchen table, her fingers tapping nervously against the wood. "We gotta stay low for a while. The cops are gonna be lookin' for us hard after this."

Bria, pacing back and forth, couldn't hide her frustration. "I can't keep doin' this, Isis. We takin' too many risks. It's only a matter of time before we get caught."

Asia, leaning against the wall, added, "Bria's right. We need to think about our next move carefully. We can't afford to slip up."

Nikki, sitting quietly in the corner, stared at her sisters, her mind racing. She had always been the most daring, but even she was starting to feel the weight of their actions. "Maybe... maybe we should lay off the heists for a while. Find another way to make money."

Isis looked at Nikki, surprised. "You the one who was all about this, Nikki. Now you wanna back out?"

Nikki shrugged, trying to keep her voice steady. "I'm just sayin', we can't keep doin' this forever. We need to find a safer way."

The room fell silent, the tension thick in the air. They had been through so much together, but the cracks were starting to show. Doubts and fears were creeping in, threatening to undermine their unity.

Later that night, as the sisters sat in their makeshift safe house, Bria approached Isis. "We need to talk," she said, her voice low.

Isis nodded, leading her to a quiet corner. "What's on your mind?"

Bria hesitated, her eyes filled with uncertainty. "I don't know if I can do this anymore, Isis. The risks, the danger... it's too much. Marcus is gettin' suspicious, and I'm scared he's gonna find out."

Isis's face softened. She knew Bria had always been the most vulnerable, caught in an abusive relationship that made everything harder. "I get it, Bria. But we need this money. For Mama, for us. We can't back out now."

Bria shook her head, tears welling in her eyes. "But what if we get caught? What if somethin' happens to us? I can't lose y'all."

Isis pulled her sister into a hug, her own fears bubbling to the surface. "We ain't gonna get caught. We just gotta be smart, stick together. We can get through this."

The sisters' bond was strong, but the strain was beginning to show. Nikki's growing doubts, Bria's fear, and the constant pressure of staying ahead of the law were taking their toll. They needed to find a way to maintain trust and unity, or risk everything falling apart.

One evening, while they were hiding out in their safe house, Tasha arrived with news. "I heard some rumors on the street. Cops are gettin' closer. They think the robbers are women."

Asia's heart sank. "Shit. We gotta be extra careful."

Tasha nodded, her face serious. "And there's more. Marcus been askin' questions. He thinks Bria's up to somethin.'"

Bria's face went pale. "I knew it. He's been actin' all paranoid. What do I do?"

Isis thought for a moment, her mind racing. "We need to keep Marcus off your trail. Make him think you ain't involved. We'll come up with a plan."

As the sisters huddled together, trying to figure out their next move, the weight of their situation pressed down on them. Trust was fragile, and any hint of betrayal could shatter everything.

The following day, Nikki met with Rico, who had become an unexpected ally. She needed someone to talk to, someone outside of her sisters who could offer a different perspective.

"I don't know if I can keep doin' this, Rico," Nikki admitted, her voice wavering. "The heists, the danger... it's too much."

Rico looked at her, his expression sympathetic. "I get it, Nikki. But you gotta stay strong for your family. If you back out now, it could all fall apart."

Nikki nodded, tears in her eyes. "I know. I just... I don't wanna lose my sisters."

Rico reached out, squeezing her hand. "You won't. You just gotta stay focused. Trust each other. That's the only way you're gonna make it through this."

As Nikki returned to the safe house, she felt a renewed sense of determination. She couldn't let her doubts tear them apart. They had to stay united, no matter the cost.

The next few days were filled with tension as they continued to lay low and plan their next move. Trust and communication became more important than ever as they navigated the treacherous path they had chosen.

One evening, as they gathered around the kitchen table, Isis addressed her sisters. "We gotta stick together. No matter what happens, we gotta have each other's backs. We did this for Mama, and we gotta see it through."

Bria, still grappling with her fears, nodded. "I'm with you, Isis. We just gotta be careful."

Asia, always the voice of reason, added, "We need to stay smart. Plan every move. We can't afford any mistakes."

Nikki, her doubts lingering but her resolve strengthening, said, "We in this together. Ride or die."

The sisters knew they had a long and dangerous road ahead. The risks were escalating, and the pressure was mounting, but they were determined to face it together. Trust was their most valuable asset, and they couldn't afford to lose it.

As they prepared for their next heist, the sisters felt the weight of their actions, but they also felt a renewed sense of unity. They had come too far to turn back now. They would face the dangers and challenges ahead with courage and determination, ready to fight for their family and their future.

The struggle was real, but so was their resolve. In the heart of the ghetto, amidst the darkness and danger, the Reed sisters were determined to rise above their circumstances and forge a new path. The road ahead was uncertain, but they would face it together, ready to take on whatever challenges lay ahead.

Chapter 9: Heist Gone Wrong

The tension in the safe house was palpable as the Reed sisters made their final preparations for the next heist. They knew the risks were higher than ever, but desperation drove them forward. Their mother's medical bills were piling up, and they needed another score to keep everything afloat. This time, the target was a high-end electronics store with a significant cash reserve and valuable merchandise.

Isis, the leader, gathered her sisters around the table, their faces illuminated by the dim light of a single bulb. "Aight, y'all. This is it. We gotta move fast and be out before the cops even know we there."

Bria, still struggling with her doubts, nodded but couldn't shake the feeling of dread. "We gotta be careful. We can't afford no mistakes."

Asia, always the cautious one, added, "We need to stick to the plan. No improvising."

Nikki, trying to keep her nerves in check, gave a small smile. "We got this. We just need to stay focused."

The sisters donned their masks and gloves, their hearts pounding with anticipation. They piled into their getaway van, Rico at the wheel, and drove silently through the darkened streets of the city. The plan was simple: break in, grab the cash and high-value items, and get out before the alarm could trigger a police response.

As they approached the store, Rico parked the van in an alley, keeping the engine running. "You got ten minutes, tops. After that, the alarm's gonna go off, and the cops will be all over this place."

Isis nodded. "We know. Let's move."

The sisters slipped out of the van and approached the back entrance of the store. Nikki, the expert lockpick, went to work, her fingers deftly manipulating the tools. The lock clicked open, and they entered the darkened store, their flashlights cutting through the darkness.

Bria and Asia moved to the front to grab the cash from the registers, while Isis and Nikki headed to the back to collect the high-value items.

The tension was thick as they worked quickly, their movements synchronized and efficient.

But then, something went wrong. The sound of a guard's footsteps echoed through the store, and panic set in. They had planned for this, but the reality of the situation was far more terrifying.

"Shit, we gotta go!" Nikki hissed, her voice trembling.

"Stay calm," Isis whispered back. "We ain't done yet."

The guard appeared, flashlight beam sweeping the room. Bria froze, her heart pounding in her chest. "We gotta take him out," she mouthed to Isis.

Isis nodded, her face grim. She crept up behind the guard and delivered a swift blow to the back of his head, knocking him out cold. But the noise was enough to trigger the alarm, and the store was suddenly filled with the blaring sound of sirens.

"Move! Now!" Isis shouted, grabbing the bags of loot.

They bolted for the back door, but as they reached the alley, they were met with flashing blue lights and the sound of police sirens closing in. Rico revved the engine, shouting, "Get in! Get in!"

The sisters piled into the van, the fear and adrenaline pumping through their veins. Rico floored the gas pedal, and they sped away, the police in hot pursuit.

As they raced through the streets, gunshots rang out, and bullets slammed into the side of the van. Nikki screamed, "We ain't gonna make it!"

"We will," Isis shouted back. "Just keep driving, Rico!"

The chase was intense, the van weaving through traffic as the police closed in. They had to lose them, or it was all over. Rico took a sharp turn into an alley, the van skidding as it narrowly missed a dumpster.

But the police were relentless. They followed, the alley echoing with the sound of sirens and screeching tires. Rico took another turn, then another, trying to lose them in the maze of backstreets.

Finally, they burst out onto a main road and saw their chance. An abandoned warehouse loomed ahead, and Rico gunned the engine, aiming for the open doors. The van shot inside, and they skidded to a stop, the heavy doors closing behind them just as the police cars roared past.

For a moment, there was silence. The sisters sat in the van, panting and trembling, their hearts pounding with the aftermath of the chase.

"We made it," Bria whispered, her voice shaky. "We actually made it."

Isis, trying to catch her breath, nodded. "But we can't stay here. We need to move. Now."

As they climbed out of the van, they heard a noise behind them. A figure stepped out of the shadows, gun drawn. It was Detective Marcus Hall, a seasoned cop with a reputation for being relentless.

"Drop the bags and put your hands up," Hall ordered, his voice cold and steady.

The sisters froze, their minds racing. They had heard of Hall, known he was one of the best. If he caught them, it was over.

Isis stepped forward, her hands raised. "We don't want no trouble, Detective. Just let us go."

Hall's eyes narrowed. "You think you can just walk away? You think I don't know who you are?"

The tension was unbearable. They had come so far, but now it seemed like it was all about to come crashing down. But then, a distraction—a loud crash from outside—drew Hall's attention for just a moment.

It was all they needed. Isis lunged forward, knocking Hall's gun aside. A struggle ensued, the sisters joining in to overpower him. They managed to disarm Hall and tied him up, but they knew their time was running out.

"We gotta move," Isis said, her voice urgent. "Rico, get the van ready."

As they piled back into the van, Hall shouted after them, "You can't run forever! I'll find you!"

The sisters drove off into the night, their hearts heavy with the knowledge that their situation had just become even more dangerous. Hall would be relentless in his pursuit, and the law was closing in.

Back at their new hideout, the reality of their situation began to sink in. They had narrowly escaped, but the stakes were higher than ever. Trust and unity were more important than ever, but the threat of betrayal and the constant pressure of staying ahead of the law weighed heavily on them.

Isis looked at her sisters, their faces etched with fear and determination. "We gotta stay strong. We can't let this tear us apart. We in this together, and we gonna get through it."

Chapter 10: Love and Lies

The Reed sisters found themselves navigating not only the dangers of their criminal enterprise but also the complexities of their personal lives. Their relationships were as volatile as the streets they ruled, and the tension was palpable.

Isis, the de facto leader, was the first to experience the complications of love and lies. Her long-time boyfriend, Malik, had always been supportive of her hustle, but lately, things had changed. Malik was becoming more controlling, more suspicious. He wanted to know where she was at all times, and the pressure was suffocating.

One night, after a particularly tense argument, Malik grabbed Isis's arm. "You think I don't know what you're up to? You think you can keep secrets from me?"

Isis yanked her arm away, her eyes blazing with anger. "I don't owe you nothin', Malik. You ain't my keeper."

The argument escalated, and Isis stormed out of the apartment, her mind racing. She knew Malik's jealousy could become a liability, but cutting him off was easier said than done. Love had a way of entangling itself in the most inconvenient places.

Meanwhile, Bria was dealing with her own relationship woes. Her boyfriend, Marcus, had always been a problem. He was abusive, manipulative, and a constant source of stress. Bria had thought about leaving him many times, but fear and love kept her anchored.

One evening, after another explosive fight, Bria found herself at a local bar, seeking solace in the bottom of a glass. That's where she met Jamal, a smooth-talking stranger with a charming smile and a listening ear. They talked for hours, and for the first time in a long time, Bria felt understood.

As the night wore on, one thing led to another, and Bria found herself in Jamal's arms, forgetting her troubles in a haze of passion. But the guilt was immediate and crushing. She had crossed a line, and the consequences would be severe.

Asia, the studious and responsible sister, was not immune to the lure of forbidden love either. She had been seeing her college professor, Mr. Lewis, for several months. Their relationship was intense and clandestine, filled with stolen moments and whispered promises. But the risk was immense.

One afternoon, as they lay tangled in each other's arms, Mr. Lewis turned to Asia, his face serious. "We can't keep doing this, Asia. If anyone finds out, we're both finished."

Asia knew he was right, but the thought of ending their relationship was unbearable. "I know it's risky, but I love you. We'll figure it out."

But love and lies were a dangerous mix, and the noose was tightening around the Reed sisters. Nikki, the youngest and most impulsive, was entangled in a relationship with a fellow hustler, Trey. Their love was passionate and fiery, but also fraught with deception.

Trey had been keeping secrets, and Nikki's suspicions were growing. One night, she followed him, her heart pounding with dread. She found him with another woman, their bodies entwined in a betrayal that cut her to the core.

Nikki confronted Trey, her voice shaking with rage. "How could you do this to me? After everything we been through?"

Trey's eyes were cold and unrepentant. "You ain't the only one with secrets, Nikki. You think I don't know about your little heists?"

The confrontation turned violent, and Nikki was left with bruises both physical and emotional. She knew she had to end things with Trey, but the ties that bound them were strong and twisted.

As the sisters struggled with their romantic entanglements, the law was closing in. Detective Marcus Hall, relentless and determined, was piecing together the clues that pointed to the Reed sisters. He was getting closer, and the pressure was mounting.

One evening, as the sisters gathered to discuss their next move, Isis shared her concerns. "The cops are getting too close. We need to lay low for a while."

Bria, her face still marked by the remnants of her recent fight with Marcus, nodded. "We can't afford any mistakes. We gotta be extra careful."

Asia, her mind occupied with thoughts of Mr. Lewis, added, "And we need to keep our personal lives out of this. No more distractions."

Nikki, nursing her wounds both seen and unseen, agreed. "We need to stay focused. No more drama."

But the drama was far from over. Their relationships were crumbling under the weight of secrets and lies, and the law was closing in. The sisters knew they had to stay united, but the cracks were beginning to show.

As the days turned into nights, the pressure intensified. Detective Hall was relentless, and the sisters could feel the walls closing in. They had to find a way to maintain their unity, or risk everything falling apart.

The stakes were higher than ever. The Reed sisters were determined to rise above their circumstances, but the road ahead was fraught with danger and deception. Love and lies were a deadly combination, and the sisters would need all their wits and courage to navigate the treacherous path ahead.

Chapter 11: Family First

The Reed sisters had always known that family came first. No matter the conflicts, betrayals, or heartaches, their loyalty to one another and their mother remained unshakable. With the law closing in and their relationships crumbling, they realized the only way to survive was to stick together.

Isis gathered her sisters in their cramped apartment, the weight of their situation evident on everyone's faces. "We gotta do this for Mama. We need one big score to set us straight, then we out for good."

Bria, nursing a bruise from her latest run-in with Marcus, nodded. "We can't keep livin' like this. It's too dangerous."

Asia, her eyes tired from sleepless nights and the stress of her secret relationship with Mr. Lewis, added, "We need to be smart about this. Plan every detail, no slip-ups."

Nikki, still recovering from her violent confrontation with Trey, clenched her fists. "Whatever it takes, we do it. For Mama."

Their mother's health had deteriorated further, and the medical bills were piling up. The sisters knew they had to pull off their biggest heist yet, hoping it would be their last. They needed the money to pay for her treatment and to secure a future away from the dangerous life they were leading.

Isis spread out the blueprint of their target: a high-profile bank downtown with lax night security. "We hit this place, we set for life. But it's risky as hell. We need to be tight, no room for error."

Bria looked at the blueprint, her heart pounding with a mix of fear and determination. "We need more help. Tasha and Rico can handle the tech and the getaway."

Asia agreed. "And we need to make sure we got eyes on the place before and during. No surprises."

Nikki, always the daredevil, smirked. "We can do this. We gotta do this."

Over the next few days, the sisters meticulously planned every detail of the heist. They studied the bank's security patterns, scouted the area for potential obstacles, and rehearsed their roles until they were second nature. Tasha and Rico were brought into the fold, their expertise invaluable in ensuring the plan's success.

As they prepared, the bond between the sisters grew stronger. They were united by a common goal and a deep love for their mother. They knew the risks were immense, but they also knew they had no choice. Failure was not an option.

The night of the heist arrived, and the tension was palpable. The sisters gathered in their hideout, dressed in black and ready to move. Isis looked at her sisters, her eyes fierce with determination. "We do this for Mama. We do this for us. We in and out, no mistakes."

Bria, her heart pounding, nodded. "We got this."

Asia, always the voice of reason, added, "Stay focused. Stick to the plan."

Nikki, her adrenaline pumping, grinned. "Let's make this count."

They piled into the getaway van, Rico at the wheel, and drove silently through the city streets. As they approached the bank, Rico parked in an alley, the engine running. "You got fifteen minutes. After that, we're out."

Isis nodded. "We know. Let's move."

The sisters slipped out of the van and approached the bank's rear entrance. Tasha, their tech expert, quickly disabled the security cameras and alarm system, allowing them entry. Inside, the bank was dimly lit, the silence broken only by the sound of their footsteps.

Isis led the way to the vault, her heart pounding. "Stick to the plan. No distractions."

Bria and Asia worked on the vault's lock, their fingers moving with practiced precision. Nikki kept watch, her eyes scanning the shadows for any sign of trouble.

As the vault door swung open, the sisters felt a surge of triumph. They began filling their bags with cash, their movements quick and efficient. But just as they were about to finish, the sound of a door creaking open froze them in their tracks.

A security guard had entered the bank, his flashlight beam sweeping the room. "Who's there?" he called out, his voice echoing in the silence.

Nikki motioned for the others to stay quiet, her heart racing. But the guard was getting closer, his flashlight illuminating the bags of money.

Isis, her mind racing, knew they had to act fast. She signaled to Tasha, who quickly pulled out a taser. The guard turned just in time to see Tasha, but before he could react, she fired, and he crumpled to the floor, unconscious.

"Let's move!" Isis whispered urgently.

They grabbed the remaining bags and made their way back to the rear entrance. As they stepped outside, the sound of distant sirens filled the air. They had to hurry.

They piled into the van, Rico flooring the gas pedal as they sped away. The tension in the van was thick, the sisters' hearts pounding with fear and adrenaline.

"We did it," Bria whispered, her voice shaking. "We actually did it."

Isis, trying to catch her breath, nodded. "But we ain't outta the woods yet. We need to lay low and get rid of this money."

They drove to their safe house, unloading the bags of cash and stashing them in a hidden compartment. The sisters sat down, their faces etched with a mix of relief and exhaustion.

"We gotta be smart about this," Asia said. "We can't just start spending the money. We need to be careful."

Nikki, her adrenaline still high, grinned. "We did good. Mama's gonna be taken care of, and we can finally get outta this life."

But Isis knew the danger was far from over. Detective Marcus Hall was relentless, and the law was closing in. They had pulled off the heist, but the true test was yet to come.

As they sat together, their bond stronger than ever, the sisters knew they had to stay united. The road ahead was uncertain, but they were determined to face it together. They had done this for their mother, for their family, and they would do whatever it took to protect each other.

In the heart of the ghetto, amidst the darkness and danger, the Reed sisters were a force to be reckoned with. They had pulled off their biggest heist yet, but the challenges were far from over. The struggle was real, but so was their resolve. They would face whatever came next, ready to fight for their family and their future.

Chapter 12: The Big Score

The night of the big score had finally arrived. The Reed sisters were ready to pull off the most dangerous and lucrative heist of their lives. They knew that this job would make or break them. Everything they had done up until now had led to this moment. The tension in the air was thick as they gathered in their hideout, going over the final details one last time.

Isis, the unflinching leader, addressed her sisters with steely resolve. "This is it, y'all. We hit this spot, we set for life. No more small-time jobs. No more runnin'. We get in, we get out, and we disappear."

Bria, her eyes reflecting a mix of fear and determination, nodded. "We gotta stick to the plan. No room for mistakes."

Asia, always the calm and collected one, added, "We need to be smart. Keep our heads on straight."

Nikki, the adrenaline junkie, grinned despite the gravity of the situation. "Let's do this."

Their target was a high-profile casino with a notoriously lax security system. The plan was to hit the casino vault during a shift change when the security guards would be at their most vulnerable. Tasha and Rico were already in position, ready to handle the tech and the getaway.

The sisters donned their black outfits, masks, and gloves, their hearts pounding with a mixture of excitement and fear. They climbed into the van, Rico at the wheel, and drove silently through the city streets, the neon lights casting an eerie glow on their determined faces.

As they approached the casino, Rico parked the van in a secluded spot, keeping the engine running. "You got twenty minutes. After that, I'm outta here."

Isis nodded. "We know. Let's move."

They slipped out of the van and approached the back entrance of the casino. Tasha, their tech genius, had already disabled the security cameras and alarm system, allowing them to enter undetected. Inside, the casino was a cacophony of flashing lights and the sounds of people gambling away their fortunes.

Isis led the way to the vault, her senses on high alert. "Stick to the plan, y'all. No distractions."

Bria and Asia moved swiftly, their eyes scanning the area for any signs of trouble. Nikki, keeping watch, felt a surge of adrenaline as she noticed a guard approaching. She quickly signaled to her sisters, her heart racing.

The guard's footsteps echoed through the corridor, and the sisters knew they had to act fast. Bria and Asia ducked into the shadows, their breath held as the guard passed by, oblivious to their presence. Once the coast was clear, they continued to the vault.

Nikki worked on the vault's lock, her fingers moving with practiced precision. The lock clicked open, and the sisters felt a surge of triumph as the door swung open, revealing stacks of cash and valuable chips. They began filling their bags, their movements quick and efficient.

But just as they were about to finish, the sound of a door creaking open froze them in their tracks. A security guard had entered the vault area, his flashlight beam sweeping the room. "Who's there?" he called out, his voice filled with suspicion.

Nikki motioned for the others to stay quiet, her heart pounding in her chest. But the guard was getting closer, his flashlight illuminating the bags of money.

Isis, her mind racing, knew they had to act fast. She signaled to Tasha, who quickly pulled out a taser. The guard turned just in time to see Tasha, but before he could react, she fired, and he crumpled to the floor, unconscious.

"Move! Now!" Isis whispered urgently.

They grabbed the remaining bags and made their way back to the rear entrance. As they stepped outside, the sound of distant sirens filled the air. They had to hurry.

They piled into the van, Rico flooring the gas pedal as they sped away. The tension in the van was thick, the sisters' hearts pounding with fear and adrenaline.

"We did it," Bria whispered, her voice shaking. "We actually did it."

Isis, trying to catch her breath, nodded. "But we ain't outta the woods yet. We need to lay low and get rid of this money."

They drove to their safe house, unloading the bags of cash and stashing them in a hidden compartment. The sisters sat down, their faces etched with a mix of relief and exhaustion.

"We gotta be smart about this," Asia said. "We can't just start spending the money. We need to be careful."

Nikki, her adrenaline still high, grinned. "We did good. Mama's gonna be taken care of, and we can finally get outta this life."

But Isis knew the danger was far from over. Detective Marcus Hall was relentless, and the law was closing in. They had pulled off the heist, but the true test was yet to come.

As they sat together, their bond stronger than ever, the sisters knew they had to stay united. The road ahead was uncertain, but they were determined to face it together. They had done this for their mother, for their family, and they would do whatever it took to protect each other.

In the heart of the ghetto, amidst the darkness and danger, the Reed sisters were a force to be reckoned with. They had pulled off their biggest heist yet, but the challenges were far from over. The struggle was real, but so was their resolve. They would face whatever came next, ready to fight for their family and their future.

The night was far from over. As they sat catching their breath, the sound of tires screeching outside made their blood run cold. Isis peered out the window, her heart sinking. "We got company," she muttered, seeing the flashing red and blue lights.

Bria's eyes widened. "How did they find us so fast?"

Asia's mind raced. "We need to get out of here. Now."

Nikki grabbed the bags of cash. "We can't leave the money behind."

Isis nodded, her face set with determination. "We'll split up. Meet at the second safe house. Go!"

They scattered, each sister taking a different route to avoid capture. The streets of the ghetto, once their home, now seemed like a maze of danger. They could hear the shouts of officers and the barking of police dogs in the distance.

Isis ran through alleyways and jumped over fences, her breath coming in short gasps. She clutched the bag of money tightly, knowing that it was their ticket to a new life. She could hear the footsteps of officers behind her, getting closer with each passing second.

Bria, her heart pounding, ducked into an abandoned building, trying to catch her breath. She knew she had to keep moving, but fear was threatening to paralyze her. She heard a noise behind her and spun around, her fists clenched.

Asia, always the calm one, used her wits to outmaneuver the officers. She slipped into a narrow alley and climbed a fire escape, her movements quick and precise. She could see the safe house in the distance, and hope surged through her veins.

Nikki, the adrenaline junkie, relished the chase. She zigzagged through the streets, her bag of cash slung over her shoulder. She knew the risks, but the thrill of the heist and the danger made her feel alive.

As the sisters raced through the city, their minds were filled with thoughts of their mother and their future. They had come too far to give up now. They had to stay one step ahead of the law, no matter what.

Finally, they reached the second safe house, their breaths coming in ragged gasps. They had made it, but just barely. The sisters collapsed on the floor, their bodies trembling with exhaustion and fear.

Isis looked at her sisters, her face etched with determination. "We can't stay here. We need to keep moving. We gotta stay ahead of the law."

Bria nodded, her eyes filled with resolve. "We'll make it. We'll find a way."

Asia, always the voice of reason, added, "We need to stick together. We can't let this break us."

Nikki, her adrenaline still pumping, grinned. "We did it. We pulled off the big score. Now we just gotta get outta this mess."

The sisters knew the road ahead was fraught with danger, but they were determined to face it together. They had pulled off their biggest heist yet, and they had each other. They would fight for their family and their future, no matter what.

As they sat in the safe house, the sound of sirens fading into the distance, they knew that their journey was far from over.

Chapter 13: On the Run

The Reed sisters were on the run. Their biggest heist had succeeded, but now the law was closing in on them fast. They had split up to avoid capture, each sister embarking on a perilous journey through the gritty streets they knew so well. The streets, once their playground, now felt like a labyrinth of danger.

Isis, always the leader, moved through the city with a mix of caution and confidence. She knew the back alleys and shortcuts better than anyone. Her first priority was to find a safe place to lay low, but every shadow seemed to harbor potential betrayal. She had to keep her wits sharp. As she slipped through the darkened streets, she heard a voice she recognized.

"Isis! Over here!" It was Tasha, their tech genius, waving her over from a shadowy corner.

"Tasha, thank God," Isis panted, catching her breath. "We gotta keep movin'. The cops are everywhere."

Tasha nodded, her face tense. "I got a place we can hide. Just follow me."

Meanwhile, Bria was navigating her own path through the urban jungle. Her mind was a whirlwind of fear and determination. She had always been the emotional one, and now those emotions threatened to overwhelm her. But she knew she couldn't afford to break down. She ducked into a rundown motel, hoping to catch a few hours of sleep and figure out her next move.

Inside the dingy room, Bria sat on the edge of the bed, her hands shaking. She needed to think clearly. Suddenly, there was a knock on the door. She tensed, ready to run, but it was Jamal, the smooth-talking stranger she had met at the bar.

"Bria, I heard about what happened. You need help?"

Bria nodded, tears welling up in her eyes. "I don't know what to do, Jamal. We pulled off the heist, but now we're running for our lives."

Jamal's expression softened. "I'll help you. But you need to trust me."

Asia, the studious and responsible sister, was using her intellect to stay ahead of the law. She had always been good at blending in, and now that skill was her best asset. She found refuge in a crowded library, burying herself in the stacks of books to avoid attention.

As she scanned the room, her eyes met those of Mr. Lewis, her college professor. He approached her, concern etched on his face. "Asia, what are you doing here? I heard about the robbery. Are you okay?"

Asia's heart raced. She had to be careful about what she revealed. "I'm fine, Mr. Lewis. Just trying to stay out of sight."

Mr. Lewis nodded. "If you need a place to stay, I can help. But you have to be honest with me."

Asia hesitated, then nodded. "I trust you. Let's go."

Nikki, always the wild card, was reveling in the adrenaline rush. She moved through the city with a mix of recklessness and cunning, always one step ahead of her pursuers. She found herself in a seedy nightclub, the music thumping and the air thick with smoke.

As she scanned the crowd, she spotted Trey, her ex-lover and fellow hustler. He approached her, a smirk on his face. "Didn't expect to see you here, Nikki. Heard you been causing quite a stir."

Nikki rolled her eyes. "Yeah, well, I ain't got time for your games, Trey. I need a place to hide."

Trey's smirk faded, replaced by a look of genuine concern. "I got a spot. Follow me."

The sisters were scattered across the city, each dealing with their own challenges. But they knew they had to regroup and figure out their next move. The law was closing in, and they couldn't afford to make any mistakes.

Isis and Tasha found refuge in an abandoned warehouse, their breaths coming in ragged gasps. "We need to get in touch with the others," Isis said, her mind racing. "We gotta find a way outta this mess."

Tasha nodded, pulling out her phone. "I'll try to reach them. But we need to be careful. The cops are monitoring everything."

Bria and Jamal were holed up in a basement apartment, the tension between them palpable. "We need to come up with a plan," Jamal said, his eyes serious. "We can't stay here forever."

Bria nodded, her mind racing. "We need to get in touch with my sisters. We can't do this alone."

Asia and Mr. Lewis found a safe house on the outskirts of the city, their breaths finally starting to even out. "Thank you," Asia said, her voice shaky. "I don't know what I would have done without you."

Mr. Lewis nodded. "We'll figure this out. But we need to be smart. The cops are looking for you."

Nikki and Trey were hiding out in an old factory, the sound of sirens echoing in the distance. "We need to lay low," Trey said, his voice tense. "The cops are everywhere."

Nikki nodded, her mind racing. "I need to get in touch with my sisters. We gotta stay together."

The Reed sisters were resourceful and determined, but they knew the road ahead was fraught with danger. They had pulled off their biggest heist yet, but now they were fugitives, each dealing with their own battles. New allies and enemies emerged, each posing a different kind of threat.

As the sisters navigated their separate paths, they knew they had to regroup and find a way out of the mess they were in. The law was relentless, and the streets were unforgiving. But they were the Reed sisters, and they would fight to the end for their family and their future.

Chapter 14: Close Calls

The Reed sisters were now fugitives, each one navigating the treacherous streets with the law breathing down their necks. Their lives had become a series of close calls, with each moment bringing them perilously close to capture. The tension was high, the danger real, and every decision could mean the difference between freedom and imprisonment.

Isis was the first to face a close call. She and Tasha were hiding in an old warehouse when they heard the sound of police sirens approaching. Panic set in as they realized the cops were closing in on their location.

"We gotta move, Tasha," Isis whispered urgently, her eyes darting around for an escape route.

Tasha nodded, her face pale with fear. "I hacked into their comms. They're sweeping the area. We need to split up."

Isis hesitated for a moment, then nodded. "You take the back exit. I'll head for the roof."

As they separated, Isis climbed the fire escape to the roof, her heart pounding in her chest. She could hear the police officers below, their radios crackling with updates. She crouched behind an air vent, praying they wouldn't look up.

Just as she thought she was safe, a beam of light from a helicopter swept across the rooftop. Isis froze, her breath caught in her throat. The light passed over her, then moved on. She let out a shaky breath and continued her escape, determined to survive.

Bria wasn't having an easier time. She and Jamal had relocated to an old friend's apartment, hoping to lay low. But it wasn't long before their location was compromised.

Jamal burst into the room, his eyes wide with alarm. "We gotta go, Bria. Cops are downstairs."

Bria's heart raced as she grabbed her bag. "How'd they find us?"

Jamal shook his head. "No time to figure that out. We need to move."

They slipped out the back door and into the alley, just as the police stormed the building. Bria's mind raced as they ran, every alley and side street a potential trap. As they rounded a corner, they nearly collided with a police officer on patrol.

Jamal reacted quickly, pulling Bria into a shadowed doorway. The officer glanced around but didn't see them. They held their breath until he moved on, then continued their escape. Bria knew they were running out of places to hide, but she refused to give up.

Asia was also on the run, using her wits to stay ahead of the law. She and Mr. Lewis had been staying in a safe house, but their luck ran out when an anonymous tip led the cops to their door.

Mr. Lewis grabbed Asia's hand. "We need to get out of here, now!"

They fled through the back door, the sound of police sirens growing louder. Asia's mind raced as they ran, her heart pounding in her chest. They reached a busy street and blended into the crowd, hoping to lose their pursuers.

As they moved through the throng of people, Asia felt a hand on her shoulder. She turned, expecting to see a police officer, but it was Mr. Lewis, his face etched with concern. "We need to split up. They're looking for two people together."

Asia nodded, tears in her eyes. "Be safe."

She slipped away into the crowd, her mind focused on staying one step ahead. She knew the danger wasn't over, but she was determined to survive.

Nikki was facing her own challenges. She and Trey had been hiding out in an abandoned factory, but their location was compromised when Trey's ex-girlfriend, jealous and spiteful, tipped off the cops.

Nikki's heart raced as she and Trey fled the building. "That bitch set us up!"

Trey gritted his teeth. "We'll deal with her later. Right now, we need to get out of here."

They ran through the streets, the sound of police sirens growing louder. Nikki's mind raced as she tried to think of a safe place to hide. They reached a dead end, and Nikki's heart sank.

"We're trapped," she whispered, panic rising in her chest.

Trey looked around, then spotted a fire escape. "Up there!"

They climbed the fire escape, their hearts pounding with fear. They reached the roof just as the police arrived below. Nikki crouched behind an air vent, her breath coming in short gasps. She could hear the officers searching the area, their voices tense.

"Split up and search the area. They're around here somewhere."

Nikki held her breath, praying they wouldn't be found. The officers moved on, and she let out a shaky breath. They were safe, for now.

Each sister was dealing with near-capture moments, the suspense and danger increasing with every step. Their resilience and determination were being tested, but they refused to give up. Betrayals, both personal and professional, added to their struggle.

Isis managed to find a temporary hideout in an abandoned building, her mind racing with plans for their next move. She knew they couldn't stay on the run forever. They needed a way out.

Bria and Jamal found refuge with a friend who owed them a favor, but Bria's mind was consumed with thoughts of her sisters. She couldn't rest until they were all safe.

Asia made her way to a library, using her skills to stay hidden and gather information. She knew they needed a new plan, and she was determined to find a way.

Nikki and Trey lay low in a different part of the city, their hearts still pounding from the close call. Nikki's mind was focused on survival, but she couldn't shake the feeling of betrayal.

As the Reed sisters navigated their separate paths, their determination and resilience shone through. They were facing incredible odds, but they refused to give up. They were fighters, survivors, and they would find a way to stay ahead of the law.

Chapter 15: The Fall

The air was thick with tension as the Reed sisters navigated their lives on the run. Each step taken, each corner turned, was fraught with the fear of capture. They had evaded the law time and time again, but their luck was running thin. The close calls were wearing on them, and the cracks were beginning to show.

Bria's capture came like a thunderclap, sudden and devastating. She had been hiding with Jamal in the basement apartment, trying to lay low and figure out their next move. The police raid happened so quickly, there was no time to react. Jamal managed to slip away, but Bria wasn't so lucky. She was dragged out in handcuffs, her face a mask of shock and fear.

Isis received the news first, a panicked call from Jamal. "They got her, Isis. They got Bria. I barely escaped. We gotta do something."

Isis's heart dropped. Bria, her sister, her blood, was now in the clutches of the law. She felt a mix of rage and helplessness. "Where did they take her?"

"Downtown. Central precinct. They're gonna book her, maybe even try to make her talk."

Isis knew Bria wouldn't talk, but the pressure would be immense. "We need to get her out. I don't care what it takes."

Asia and Nikki were quickly informed. Asia's eyes were wide with fear, while Nikki's face was set with a grim determination. "We can't let them break her," Nikki said, her voice low and fierce. "We have to get her out."

The emotional impact was heavy. They were a team, a family, and now one of their own was behind bars. The pressure to turn themselves in, to try and negotiate for Bria's release, was intense, but they knew it was a gamble. The law would show no mercy.

Asia, always the planner, started to map out their options. "We can't just walk in there. We need a plan, something bold, something they won't see coming."

Isis nodded, her mind racing. "We'll need help. We can't do this alone."

They reached out to their allies, those who owed them favors, those who were willing to risk everything for them. Tasha and Rico were first to step up. "We're in," Tasha said, her eyes determined. "Whatever you need."

Rico nodded. "This is gonna be dangerous, but we got your back."

The plan began to take shape. They would create a diversion, something big enough to draw the attention of the entire precinct, while a smaller team would infiltrate and extract Bria. It was risky, but they had no other choice.

As they prepared, the sisters grappled with their emotions. Isis felt the weight of leadership, the responsibility of making sure they all made it out alive. Asia battled her fear, knowing that one wrong move could cost them everything. Nikki's anger burned hot, fueling her determination to see this through.

The night of the rescue arrived. The tension was palpable as they took their positions. Tasha and Rico were in place, ready to create the diversion. Isis, Asia, and Nikki waited in the shadows, their hearts pounding in unison.

"Ready?" Isis whispered, her voice barely audible.

Asia and Nikki nodded. "Let's do this."

Tasha and Rico made their move, setting off a series of explosions in the parking lot. The noise was deafening, and chaos erupted as police officers rushed to contain the situation. The sisters took advantage of the distraction, slipping into the building unnoticed.

Inside, the air was thick with smoke and confusion. They moved quickly, using the layout Tasha had provided to navigate the corridors. They reached the holding cells, their hearts racing.

Bria was there, looking small and scared behind the bars. When she saw her sisters, her eyes filled with tears. "I knew you'd come."

Isis worked quickly to pick the lock, her fingers steady despite the adrenaline coursing through her veins. The lock clicked open, and Bria stumbled out, falling into her sisters' arms.

"We need to move," Asia urged, her voice tense. "They'll be back any minute."

They retraced their steps, their movements swift and silent. As they neared the exit, the sound of approaching footsteps made their blood run cold. They ducked into a storage closet, holding their breath as officers passed by.

When the coast was clear, they made their final dash to freedom. The explosions had subsided, but the chaos was still in full swing. They slipped out of the building and into the night, their hearts pounding with relief and fear.

Rico was waiting with the van, his face etched with worry. "Let's get the hell out of here."

They piled into the van, the tension finally breaking as they drove away. Bria was safe, but they knew the danger was far from over. The law would double down on their efforts to capture them, and they had just made themselves the most wanted fugitives in the city.

As they drove through the dark streets, the sisters clung to each other, their bond stronger than ever. They had pulled off the impossible, but the road ahead was fraught with peril. They knew they couldn't stop now. They had to keep moving, keep fighting, and stay one step ahead of the law.

Chapter 16: The Final Stand

The Reed sisters knew that this was it. The final stand. The showdown they had been dreading and preparing for in equal measure. The air was thick with tension, a tangible electricity that crackled around them as they geared up for the fight of their lives. Each sister carried the weight of their family's survival on their shoulders, knowing that this confrontation would decide everything.

Isis, the eldest and the leader, stood at the forefront, her eyes steely and determined. "We end this tonight. No more running. No more hiding. We take the fight to them."

Nikki, always the wildcard, grinned, a feral gleam in her eye. "Damn right. Let's show these fools who they're messing with."

Bria, recently rescued and still bruised from her capture, nodded fiercely. "For Mama. For our family. We do this."

Asia, the quiet strategist, checked her weapon one last time. "Stick to the plan. We have to be smart about this."

They moved through the darkened streets, each step purposeful and silent. The city was their battlefield, the ghetto their arena. They had chosen an old, abandoned warehouse as the location for the final showdown. It was neutral territory, a place where they could use their intimate knowledge of the environment to their advantage.

As they approached the warehouse, they could see the lights of their enemies' vehicles cutting through the darkness. The rival gang, led by Darnell "D-Bo" Johnson, was already there, waiting. They were a formidable force, ruthless and heavily armed. But the Reed sisters had something more powerful: a bond forged in blood, sweat, and tears.

The confrontation began with a tense standoff. D-Bo stepped forward, his eyes cold and calculating. "So, the Reed sisters finally show up. Thought y'all would keep running."

Isis stepped forward, her gaze unwavering. "We ain't running no more, D-Bo. This ends tonight."

D-Bo chuckled, a sinister sound. "Brave words. Let's see if you can back them up."

The first shot rang out, piercing the silence and igniting the chaos. The warehouse erupted into a battlefield, gunfire echoing off the walls, the smell of gunpowder thick in the air. The sisters moved with precision and purpose, their every action a testament to their determination to survive.

Nikki was a blur of motion, her wild energy driving her forward as she took down one enemy after another. She relished the fight, her grin widening with every victory. But it was more than just adrenaline; it was the desperate need to protect her family.

Bria fought with a ferocity fueled by recent trauma. She was a force of nature, her pain and anger channeled into every punch, every shot fired. She had been through hell, and she was determined to ensure her family never suffered like that again.

Asia, the strategist, moved with calculated precision. She anticipated her enemies' moves, outsmarting them at every turn. Her calm exterior belied the storm within, a storm that drove her to fight harder, smarter, better.

Isis, the leader, was everywhere at once. She coordinated their efforts, her voice steady and commanding despite the chaos. Her heart ached with the weight of responsibility, but she knew she couldn't falter. Not now. Not when they were so close.

The battle raged on, a cacophony of violence and desperation. The sisters took hits, but they kept going, driven by the unyielding need to protect each other and their mother. The warehouse became a war zone, bodies falling, blood spilling, but the Reed sisters stood strong.

In a moment of brutal clarity, Isis faced D-Bo. Their eyes locked, a silent understanding passing between them. This was it. The endgame. They fought with a savagery born of necessity, each knowing that only one would walk away.

D-Bo was strong, ruthless, but Isis had something he lacked: a reason to fight beyond herself. She moved with purpose, her strikes precise and devastating. With a final, decisive blow, she brought D-Bo to his knees, ending the reign of their most dangerous enemy.

As the dust settled, the sisters gathered, bruised and bloodied but alive. The warehouse was silent now, the echoes of the battle fading into the night. They had done it. They had survived.

They returned home, their mother waiting anxiously. The sight of her daughters, victorious but scarred, brought tears to her eyes. They had fought for her, for their family, and they had won.

In the days that followed, the Reed sisters began to piece their lives back together. The streets still held danger, but they were no longer running. They were rebuilding, reclaiming their future.

Isis looked out over the city one evening, the skyline a mix of hope and history. "We did it," she murmured. "We survived."

Nikki joined her, a grin on her face. "And we'll keep surviving. Together."

Bria and Asia nodded, their expressions resolute. The fight wasn't over, but they were ready for whatever came next.

In the heart of the ghetto, amidst the shadows and the struggle, the Reed sisters had proven their strength. They had faced their enemies, confronted their fears, and emerged victorious. Their journey was far from over, but they faced the future with unbreakable resolve.

The final stand had tested them, but it had also forged them into something stronger. They were survivors, fighters, and together, they would face whatever challenges lay ahead. The Reed sisters were ready for anything.

Chapter 17: Consequences

The aftermath of the final stand left the Reed sisters battered but unbroken. The victory was theirs, but the cost was high. The warehouse was littered with the evidence of their desperate battle: broken glass, spent shells, and the bodies of those who had fallen. The sisters stood together in the cold light of dawn, each bearing the marks of their struggle.

Isis looked around at her sisters, her face a mask of exhaustion and determination. "We did it," she said, her voice barely more than a whisper. "But we ain't done yet."

Nikki, always the fighter, nodded. "We took out D-Bo, but the cops are gonna be all over this. We need to move, and we need to move fast."

Bria, still feeling the sting of her capture, winced as she looked at her bruised hands. "We need a plan. We can't just keep running forever."

Asia, the strategist, already had an idea forming. "We need to disappear. Not just lay low—completely vanish. But before we do that, we need to make sure Mama is safe."

Their mother had been their anchor through the storm. The thought of her suffering more because of their actions was unbearable. They had fought for her, for their family, and now they needed to ensure her safety above all else.

As they gathered their belongings and prepared to leave the warehouse, they heard the distant sound of sirens. Law enforcement was closing in, drawn by the chaos of the night. Isis's mind raced. They couldn't be caught now, not after everything they had been through.

"We need to split up," Isis said, her tone decisive. "We'll regroup at the safe house Tasha set up for us. Move fast and stay low."

They scattered, each sister taking a different route through the city. Isis knew the police would be scouring the area, looking for any trace of them. She moved with purpose, her mind focused on the next steps.

They had one last trick up their sleeve—a plan to buy them enough time to disappear completely.

As Isis reached the rendezvous point, she found Tasha waiting with a van. "We need to make a diversion," Isis said as she climbed in. "Something big enough to throw the cops off our trail."

Tasha nodded, her fingers already flying over her laptop. "I've got just the thing. There's a construction site nearby. We can use it to create a controlled explosion. It'll draw every cop in the area."

Isis felt a surge of gratitude. Tasha had been their lifeline, always one step ahead. "Do it," she said. "We need to give the others time to get here."

The explosion rocked the city, a massive fireball lighting up the sky. The sirens grew louder as police and emergency services rushed to the scene. Isis knew they had only a small window of time to make their escape.

One by one, the sisters arrived at the safe house, each bearing the marks of their battle. Nikki's knuckles were bloodied, Bria's face was pale from exhaustion, and Asia's eyes were sharp with determination. They had made it, but the danger was far from over.

"We need to get Mama out of here," Bria said, her voice trembling. "She can't stay in the city. It's too dangerous."

Isis nodded. "We'll take her to Auntie Rose's place in the country. It's off the grid. No one will think to look for her there."

The community's reaction to the battle was mixed. Some saw the sisters as heroes, taking down a dangerous gang and protecting their neighborhood. Others saw them as criminals, a blight on the community. The power dynamics were shifting, and the sisters knew they had to be careful.

As they prepared to leave the city, they couldn't shake the feeling that they were being watched. Law enforcement was closing in, and they needed to stay ahead of the game. But they had one last card to play—a plan that would ensure their safety and their mother's.

"We need to create new identities," Asia said, her mind working through the details. "I've been working on it for a while. We can slip away, start over somewhere new."

Nikki looked skeptical. "And what about the cops? They're not gonna just let us go."

Asia's eyes were steely. "We make them think we're dead. The explosion, the chaos—we can use it to our advantage. Leave behind enough evidence to make it look like we didn't make it out."

Isis felt a pang of fear. It was a risky plan, but it might be their only chance. "Let's do it," she said. "For Mama. For our future."

The sisters set the plan in motion, each step meticulously planned. They created the illusion of their deaths, planting evidence and making sure the explosion's aftermath covered their tracks. It was a dangerous game, but they had no other choice.

As they watched the news report the next day, they saw the police confirm their deaths. The Reed sisters were officially off the radar, free to start their new lives.

But the journey wasn't over. They had new identities, new challenges, and a new future to build. They would always carry the scars of their past, but they were survivors. They had faced the darkness and emerged stronger.

The Reed sisters were ready for their new beginning, but they knew the streets never truly let go. They would always be watching, always be prepared. Their story was far from over, and they were ready for whatever came next.

The final stand had tested them, but it had also forged them into something unbreakable.

Chapter 18: New Beginnings

The sun rose over the new horizon of the Reed sisters' lives, casting a soft glow that signaled both an end and a beginning. The journey they had endured was etched into their souls, every hardship a chapter in their story of survival and resilience. The sisters sat together in their new home, a modest house far from the chaos of their past, each one lost in thoughts of the battles they had fought and the lessons they had learned.

Isis leaned back, staring out the window at the peaceful surroundings. "We made it," she said softly, her voice tinged with both disbelief and relief. "I can't believe we actually made it."

Nikki, ever the firebrand, smirked. "You sound surprised, sis. We always knew we had it in us. Just had to show the world."

Bria, her eyes filled with a mix of sorrow and hope, nodded. "But it wasn't easy. We lost so much along the way. Friends, trust... our innocence."

Asia, the planner, looked thoughtful. "Every step, every decision—it all led us here. We're stronger now, smarter. But we can't forget where we came from or what we did to survive."

Their mother, now recovering in their new home, smiled weakly from her bed. "My girls. You fought so hard. I'm proud of you all, but I worry about what this life has done to you."

The sisters knew their mother had a point. The streets had left their mark, a permanent reminder of the price they had paid. But they also knew that they had emerged from the darkness with a renewed sense of purpose and unity.

Isis stood up, her gaze steady. "We've come a long way, but this is just the beginning. We need to build something better, not just for us but for everyone we've left behind."

Nikki nodded, her eyes gleaming with determination. "Yeah, we owe it to them. To all the people who didn't make it out."

Bria glanced at her sisters, a smile forming on her lips. "And we will. Together, we can do anything."

Asia added, "We need to make sure the next generation doesn't have to go through what we did. We can use what we've learned to make a real difference."

As they talked about their plans for the future, the doorbell rang. Isis tensed, but Nikki motioned for her to relax. "I'll get it."

Nikki opened the door to find Rico and Tasha standing there, their faces a mixture of relief and happiness. "Thought you'd be halfway to Mexico by now," Rico joked.

Tasha hugged Nikki tightly. "We just wanted to make sure you were safe. That everything worked out."

Isis smiled as she joined them at the door. "We're good. Thanks to you both. We couldn't have done it without you."

Rico nodded. "You girls are like family. We're just glad you're okay."

The group sat down to catch up, sharing stories and laughter that felt almost foreign after so much turmoil. The sense of camaraderie was palpable, a testament to the bonds forged in the fires of adversity.

But not everyone found redemption. News came through that D-Bo's remaining lieutenants had been rounded up by the police. The power vacuum left by his fall had sparked a brutal gang war, leading to more arrests and casualties. The streets were still dangerous, a constant reminder that their past was never far behind.

Asia looked at the news report, her expression somber. "The streets never let go, do they?"

Isis shook her head. "No, they don't. But we can rise above them. We have to."

As evening fell, the sisters sat around a fire pit in their backyard, the flames casting flickering shadows on their faces. Each one reflected on their journey, the sacrifices they had made, and the people they had lost.

Isis thought about all the decisions that had led them to this point. She felt the weight of leadership, but also the pride of having guided her sisters through the darkest times. She knew they still had battles to fight, but they were ready.

Nikki, her ever-defiant spirit unbroken, knew she had to channel her energy into something positive. The streets had taught her to fight, and now she would fight for something better. She was ready to protect her family and build a new future.

Bria, who had faced the brutality of betrayal and capture, found strength in her vulnerability. She knew she had grown from her experiences and was determined to use her knowledge to help others avoid the same pitfalls.

Asia, the planner and thinker, was already mapping out their next steps. She knew they needed to be smart, to stay one step ahead. But she also knew that they could create something beautiful from the ashes of their past.

As the night deepened, Isis spoke, her voice filled with quiet determination. "This is our new beginning. We may never fully escape the shadows of our past, but we can build something better. For us, for Mama, for everyone who looks up to us."

The sisters nodded, each one feeling the truth of her words. They had survived the streets, faced down their enemies, and come out stronger. The journey had been long and hard, but it had also forged them into warriors, ready to take on whatever challenges lay ahead.

The Reed sisters had found their new beginning. The road ahead was uncertain, but they knew they would face it together, their bond unbreakable. The streets had tried to break them, but they had risen above, ready to write the next chapter of their lives. Together, they would create a future where hope and resilience triumphed over darkness and despair.

Chapter 19: Closure

The streets of their past were far behind them, but the echoes of those days remained. Each of the Reed sisters found herself at a crossroads, seeking closure and new beginnings in their own ways. The journey had scarred them, shaped them, but it had also given them the strength to carve out their own futures.

Isis, always the pillar of strength, decided to channel her leadership into something legitimate. She opened a community center in their new neighborhood, a safe haven for at-risk youth. She knew firsthand the allure of the streets and wanted to offer a different path. The center provided tutoring, counseling, and job training, a lifeline for those who might otherwise fall through the cracks.

On opening day, the center buzzed with activity. Kids played basketball, teens worked on computers, and parents chatted over coffee. Isis walked through the halls, her heart swelling with pride and purpose. She paused to watch a group of girls in a self-defense class, remembering how she had fought to protect her sisters.

A familiar face appeared in the doorway. Rico, looking out of place but determined, stepped inside. "Thought I'd come see what all the fuss is about."

Isis smiled. "Glad you did. We're making a difference, Rico. One step at a time."

Rico nodded, his expression softening. "You're doing good, Isis. Real good."

Meanwhile, Nikki embraced her rebellious spirit but steered it into a new direction. She found work as a bounty hunter, tracking down those who had slipped through the cracks of the justice system. It was dangerous, thrilling, and it allowed her to stay on the edge without crossing the line.

Her first big case was a high-stakes chase through the city, ending in a dramatic showdown. Nikki cornered her target in an abandoned warehouse, the very place that had once been their battlefield. The adrenaline surged as she cuffed him, the satisfaction of a job well done coursing through her veins.

"Not so tough now, are you?" she muttered, hauling him to his feet.

As the police arrived to take the man into custody, Nikki couldn't help but feel a sense of closure. She had found a way to fight, to protect, without losing herself to the darkness.

Bria, ever the nurturer, focused on rebuilding her personal life. She reconnected with Jamal, who had stayed by her side through thick and thin. They moved to a small town, far from the chaos of the city, and started fresh. Bria enrolled in nursing school, determined to turn her experiences into something positive.

One evening, as Bria sat on the porch of their new home, Jamal joined her, handing her a cup of tea. "You've come a long way, Bria."

She smiled, her heart full. "We both have. And we're just getting started."

Asia, the planner, took her skills into the corporate world. She landed a job with a security firm, using her knowledge of strategy and risk management to help businesses protect themselves. It was a far cry from the life she had known, but it felt right.

One day, as Asia reviewed security protocols for a high-profile client, she received a call from Tasha. "Just checking in, making sure you're not getting too boring over there."

Asia laughed. "Don't worry, Tasha. I still get my thrills. Just in a different way now."

Tasha's voice softened. "I'm proud of you, Asia. You've turned it all around."

The sisters stayed close, their bond unbreakable. They met regularly, supporting each other through the ups and downs of their new lives. The scars of their past were still there, but they wore them with pride, a testament to their resilience.

One evening, they gathered at Isis's community center, reminiscing about their journey. The center was bustling, filled with laughter and hope. As they watched the kids play, the weight of their past seemed lighter.

"We've come so far," Isis said, her voice filled with emotion. "But we couldn't have done it without each other."

Nikki nodded. "We survived because we stuck together. That's what family does."

Bria squeezed her sisters' hands. "No matter where life takes us, we'll always have this. We'll always have each other."

Asia looked around the room, her heart swelling with pride. "And we'll keep making a difference. For Mama, for everyone we've lost. We'll keep fighting."

Their mother, now healthy and strong, joined them, wrapping her arms around her daughters. "You've all made me so proud. You've turned your pain into something beautiful."

The sisters knew their journey was far from over. The streets had tried to break them, but they had risen above, stronger and more united than ever. Their new beginnings were filled with hope, but they remained vigilant, always aware of the shadows that lingered.

As they stood together, the future stretched out before them, filled with endless possibilities. They had found closure, but they knew the fight for a better life was ongoing. Together, they would face whatever came next, their bond unbreakable, their spirits unyielding.

The Reed sisters had emerged from the darkness, ready to write the next chapter of their lives. The streets might never truly let go, but they had found their strength, their purpose, and their hope. They were survivors, warriors, and together, they would create a future where love, resilience, and unity triumphed over all.

Chapter 20: Legacy

The legacy of the Reed sisters' journey was felt far and wide, reverberating through their community and leaving an indelible mark on their family. The streets, which had once threatened to consume them, now bore witness to their resilience and strength. The sisters had emerged from the darkness, each finding a path that honored their shared past and looked toward a brighter future.

Isis's community center had become a beacon of hope in their neighborhood. The center thrived, offering opportunities and support to those who needed it most. The kids who once roamed aimlessly now had a safe space to learn, grow, and dream. Isis watched them with pride, knowing that her efforts were making a tangible difference.

One afternoon, as she stood at the entrance of the center, a young girl approached her. "Miss Isis, can you help me with my homework?"

Isis smiled warmly, kneeling to the girl's level. "Of course, sweetheart. Let's see what you've got."

Her interactions with the children filled her with a sense of purpose. She had turned her pain into a driving force for good, ensuring that others wouldn't have to walk the same dangerous paths she and her sisters had.

Nikki's bounty hunting career had gained her respect and notoriety. She was known for her tenacity and effectiveness, but also for her unyielding code of honor. She only took jobs that aligned with her sense of justice, refusing to sell out for a quick buck.

During a particularly tough case, Nikki tracked a fugitive to an abandoned building. The man was desperate and armed, but Nikki's fearlessness saw her through. She disarmed him and brought him in, feeling a sense of closure with each capture. She had found a way to fight without losing herself to the chaos of the streets.

Bria's new life with Jamal was a testament to her determination to start over. Nursing school had been challenging, but Bria faced each hurdle with the same grit that had seen her through the darkest times. She had found joy in helping others heal, turning her own suffering into empathy and care.

One night, as she returned home from a late shift, she found Jamal waiting for her with a candlelit dinner. "What's all this?" she asked, surprised.

Jamal took her hand, his eyes full of love and pride. "I just wanted to show you how much you mean to me. You've worked so hard, Bria. I'm proud of you."

Tears welled in Bria's eyes. She had fought for this, for a chance at happiness. And now, she was living it.

Asia's career in corporate security had flourished. She used her strategic mind to protect businesses from threats, earning respect and recognition in her field. Yet, she never forgot where she came from. She used her success to give back, funding scholarships and programs for disadvantaged youth.

At a gala honoring her contributions, Asia stood at the podium, looking out at the audience. "Everything I've achieved is because of the lessons I learned growing up. My sisters and I faced challenges that could have broken us, but we turned our struggles into strength. This is just the beginning. Together, we can build a future where no one is left behind."

The applause was thunderous, but Asia's thoughts were with her sisters. They had survived together, and their bond remained unbreakable.

The sisters gathered frequently, their laughter and stories filling the air with warmth and nostalgia. One evening, they decided to visit the old neighborhood, to see how far they had come. As they walked the familiar streets, memories flooded back—both good and bad.

Standing in front of their childhood home, Isis spoke softly. "We've come a long way, haven't we?"

Nikki nodded. "Damn right we have. And we did it together."

Bria looked at the house, her eyes misty. "It wasn't always easy, but we made it. We're stronger because of it."

Asia added, "And we'll keep moving forward. For Mama, for each other, and for everyone who looks up to us."

Their mother joined them, her presence a comforting anchor. "You've made me proud every step of the way. You've turned your pain into power, your struggles into success."

The final scene of their visit was poignant. As they stood in the fading light, they knew that their legacy was one of survival and resilience. The streets had tried to break them, but they had risen above, transforming their experiences into a force for good.

The Reed sisters had faced their demons, conquered their fears, and built a future that honored their past. Their bond, forged in the fires of adversity, remained strong and unyielding. They had created a legacy that would inspire others to rise above their circumstances, to fight for a better life.

As they walked away from their old home, the sisters knew that their journey was far from over. They had new challenges to face, new dreams to chase, but they would do it together. Their legacy was one of strength, resilience, and unbreakable unity. The streets might never truly let go, but the Reed sisters had proven that they could rise above, creating a future where hope and determination triumphed over all.

Don't miss out!

Visit the website below and you can sign up to receive emails whenever Rachael Reed publishes a new book. There's no charge and no obligation.

https://books2read.com/r/B-A-WXARB-XRVPD

BOOKS2READ

Connecting independent readers to independent writers.

Did you love *Get Money Girls*? Then you should read *Cartel Bloodline*[1] by Rachael Reed!

[2]

Cartel Bloodline: A Tale of Love, Betrayal, and Survival in the Miami Underworld

In the ruthless streets of Miami, where the Cartel controls eighty percent of the cocaine flowing through the port, power is everything, and trust is a luxury no one can afford. When the most feared gangster, Antonio Brown, falls, he leaves behind a legacy that's more explosive than anyone could've imagined. His death unearths a hidden secret—an illegitimate son, Antonio Lewis, who's about to step into a world where loyalty is bought with blood and betrayal lurks around every corner.

Antonio Lewis, raised far from the chaos of Miami's underworld, gets pulled into the Cartel's deadly embrace when he learns of his father's

---

1. https://books2read.com/u/4jpKMk

2. https://books2read.com/u/4jpKMk

empire. Thrown into a cutthroat game where every ally is a potential enemy, Antonio must navigate the treacherous waters of his father's legacy, battling for his place in the empire while uncovering the dark secrets that threaten to consume him.

Lea, a deadly beauty with a heart of steel, leads The Get Money Girls, a crew of contract killers who live by their own rules. When her cousin falls in a botched hit on the Cartel, Lea vows revenge, unaware that her heart would soon become entangled with the enemy. Antonio and Lea's worlds collide in a storm of passion and deceit, their forbidden love a ticking time bomb ready to explode.

As alliances crumble and enemies close in, Antonio and Lea must face the ultimate betrayal from within their ranks. The lines between love and loyalty blur, and survival becomes a deadly game of cat and mouse. The streets of Miami become a battlefield, where every decision could mean life or death, and the only way out is to fight until the last breath.

Will Antonio rise to claim his father's throne, or will the legacy of the Cartel drag him down into the abyss? Can Lea reconcile her thirst for vengeance with the love that binds her to Antonio, or will the secrets they uncover tear them apart forever?

Cartel Bloodline is a gritty, suspense-filled journey through the dark underbelly of Miami, where power is fleeting, love is dangerous, and the ultimate betrayal could come from the person you trust the most. In this world, nothing is as it seems, and the streets never forget.

Also by Rachael Reed

Codefendant
Codefendant
Once a Cheater
Once a Cheater
Passport Bro
What Happens in Prison
Preference
Sprinkle Sprinkle
Championship Bad
Street Exodus
Street Exodus
Street Royalty
Pawns of Power
SIS
Cartel Bloodline
Get Money Girls

www.ingramcontent.com/pod-product-compliance
Lightning Source LLC
Chambersburg PA
CBHW031501130726
47989CB00003B/1501